REDEFINING CANADA: A DEVELOPING IDENTITY
1960-1984

TITLE LIST

REDEFINING CANADA: A DEVELOPING IDENTITY
1960-1984

BY
SHEILA NELSON

MASON CREST PUBLISHERS
PHILADELPHIA

Mason Crest Publishers Inc.
370 Reed Road
Broomall, Pennsylvania 19008
(866) MCP-BOOK (toll free)

First printing
1 2 3 4 5 6 7 8 9 10

Library of Congress Cataloging-in-Publication Data

Nelson, Sheila.
  Redefining Canada : a developing identity, 1960–1984 / by Sheila Nelson.
      p. cm. — (How Canada became Canada)
  Includes index.
  ISBN 1-4222-0008-6   ISBN 1-4222-0000-0 (series)
  1. Canada—History—1945—Juvenile literature. 2. National characteristics, Canadian—Juvenile literature. 3.
Canada—Politics and government—1945–1980—Juvenile literature. I. Title.
  F1034.2.N413 2006
  971.06—dc22
                              2005013715

Produced by Harding House Publishing Service, Inc.
www.hardinghousepages.com
Interior design by MK Bassett-Harvey.
Cover design by Dianne Hodack.
Printed in Hashemite Kingdom of Jordan.

CONTENTS

INTRODUCTION

by David Bercuson

Every country's history is distinct, and so is Canada's. Although Canada is often said to be a pale imitation of the United States, it has a unique history that has created a modern North American nation on its own path to democracy and social justice. This series explains how that happened.

Canada's history is rooted in its climate, its geography, and in its separate political development. Virtually all of Canada experiences long, dark, and very cold winters with copious amounts of snowfall. Canada also spans several distinct geographic regions, from the rugged western mountain ranges on the Pacific coast to the forested lowlands of the St. Lawrence River Valley and the Atlantic tidewater region.

Canada's regional divisions were complicated by the British conquest of New France at the end of the Seven Years' War in 1763. Although Britain defeated France, the French were far more numerous in Canada than the British. Britain was thus forced to recognize French Canadian rights to their own language, religion, and culture. That recognition is now enshrined in the Canadian Constitution. It has made Canada a democracy that values group rights alongside individual rights, with official French/English bilingualism as a key part of the Canadian character.

During the American Revolution, Canadians chose to stay British. After the Revolution, they provided refuge to tens of thousands of Americans who, for one reason or another, did not follow George Washington, Benjamin Franklin, or the other founders of the United States who broke with Britain.

Democracy in Canada under the British Crown evolved more slowly than it did in the United States. But in the early nineteenth century, slavery was outlawed in the

British Empire, and as a result, also in Canada. Thus Canada never experienced civil war or government-imposed racial segregation.

From these few, brief examples, it is clear that Canada's history differs considerably from that of the United States. And yet today, Canada is a true North American democracy in its own right. Canadians will profit from a better understanding of how their country was shaped—and Americans may learn much about their own country by studying the story of Canada.

The Liberal Party's logo

One

THE BEGINNING OF CHANGE

For years, Maurice Duplessis and his Union Nationale party ruled Québec. Under Duplessis, Québec's traditional values were strong, and the Roman Catholic Church supported the Union Nationale. When time came for elections, Catholic priests would point to the blue colors of the Union Nationale next to the red emblem of the Liberal Party and proclaim, *"Le ciel est bleu; l'enfer est rouge!"*—Heaven is blue; hell is red!

After Duplessis died in September of 1959, and his *successor* died after less than four months in office, the Union Nationale fell into disorder. When *provincial* elections were held in Québec on June 22, 1960, Jean Lesage of the Québec Liberal Party campaigned with the slogan *"Il faut que ça change!"*—Things have got to change! The people of Québec agreed, and the Liberals took control of the province.

A *successor* is someone who follows another person into office.

Something that is *provincial* belongs to or comes from a province.

The Quiet Revolution

The 1960s were a time of great change in Canada and throughout the world. New technologies and scientific discoveries changed the way people thought about the world where they lived. The baby boomers, the generation of children born to returning World War II soldiers, were growing up with new ideas, questioning their parents' social structures.

In Québec, these changes were much more dramatic than in the rest of Canada. Under Maurice Duplessis, Québec had little unemployment and no provincial debt, but it had also limited personal freedoms, and its system of *patronage* favored Duplessis's friends and political allies.

Duplessis feared the spread of *communism*, and instituted the Padlock Law in 1937 to work against communist groups in Québec. Under the Padlock Law, the doors

Maurice Duplessis

Jean Lesage

to any building merely suspected of being used as a gathering place by communists could be chained shut without proof of guilt. Duplessis used the law to harass labor unions as well as known communist groups. Years after Duplessis's death, the Supreme Court of Canada finally declared the Padlock Law unconstitutional.

Not all of Duplessis's actions were negative. He did work to gain greater provincial rights for Québec and introduced the Québec provincial flag, the *Fleurdelisé*. However, many criticized him for selling Québec's natural resources to American businesses.

When Jean Lesage and the Québec Liberal Party took power, a period of reform began in Québec, leaving behind the old ways of Maurice Duplessis. Lesage worked quickly: during his first weeks in office, he often introduced a new project every day. He restructured Québec's education system, **nationalized** electricity production, **unionized** the civil service, and took steps to introduce programs such as pension plans, provincial health care, and a welfare system. Seemingly overnight, Québec rejected many of the traditional values it had held for centuries. No longer was the Roman Catholic Church the pillar of society. No longer did people highly value the rural way of life; agriculture became less important and birth rates dropped. Most important, Québec developed a new sense of identity; the people of Québec began to think of themselves as *Québécois*, unique and distinct from English Canada.

The rest of Canada was making similar changes at the same time, but Québec had further to go to catch up with the rest of the nation. The speed of change amazed Canadians, who began referring to Lesage's reforms as Québec's "Quiet Revolution." The changes were certainly revolutionary.

Patronage refers to the appointments or privileges that a politician can give to loyal supporters.

Communism is an economic theory in which there is a classless society and a working-class revolution gives ownership and control of wealth and property to the state.

If something is national-ized, control of it has been transferred from the private sector to government control or ownership.

Unionized means that workers have been organized into labor unions.

*If something is **secular**, it is not controlled by a religious body or concerned with religious or spiritual matters.*

***Nationalism** is a proud loyalty and devotion to a nation.*

*A **Marxist** believes in Marxism, the political and economic theory in which class struggle is central to the analysis of social change in Western societies.*

*A **manifesto** is a written public declaration of principles, policies, and objectives, especially one issued by a political movement or candidate.*

***Supersonic** means faster than the speed of sound.*

Women's rights were strengthened, the province became increasingly **secular**, and a new sense of **nationalism** grew rapidly. The Québécois looked back on Maurice Duplessis's time in office, only a few years earlier, shook their heads, and called those years *La grande noirceur*—the Great Darkness.

The Birth of the FLQ

The Quiet Revolution sparked a movement in Québec that was neither quiet nor peaceful. The increased sense of identity led some Québécois to believe the province should separate from the rest of Canada and form an independent country. In 1963, a separatist group formed called *Le Front de Libération du Québec* (FLQ). The FLQ was a **Marxist** group that believed in radical measures to fulfill their ideals. In April of 1963, they issued a **manifesto** claiming "the Québécois people have had enough of submitting to Anglo-Saxon capitalism."

Members of the FLQ—called *Felquistes*—began a series of attacks against English-speaking residents of Montréal. They planted bombs in mailboxes, held up banks with machine guns, and tossed incendiaries into factories and military buildings. Many of the original Felquistes were arrested and imprisoned within a year. The FLQ operated in small cells, however, and several cells continued to exist in Québec throughout the 1960s.

Lester Pearson Becomes Prime Minister

In 1963, Canadians voted in a general election to decide whether or not they wanted John Diefenbaker to continue as

The FLQ's flag

prime minister. Diefenbaker had become prime minister in 1957, bringing the Progressive Conservative Party into power, but he had made several controversial decisions during his years in office. He had cancelled the Avro Arrow project, for example, a *supersonic* fighter jet intended to be used to intercept Soviet fighters in the Arctic. He cut the program because of its enormous expense, but many Canadians felt the choice hurt Canada's standing in the international community. He also distrusted Americans

The **Cuban Missile Crisis** *was a conflict between the Soviet Union and the United States over the Soviet placement of nuclear missiles in Cuba.*

Volatile *means characterized by or prone to sudden change.*

Apartheid *was a political system in South Africa from 1948 to the early 1990s that separated people living there by race and ethnic origin.*

and especially disliked American president John F. Kennedy. When Kennedy, facing the **Cuban Missile Crisis** in 1962, asked Canada to put its military on high alert, Diefenbaker stalled for several days, not wanting to appear to be pushed around by the Americans.

Diefenbaker had a *volatile* personality. At times, he tended to follow his emotions rather than logic. This led him to things such as introducing the Canadian Bill of Rights and to

Nuclear missiles

opposing *apartheid* in South Africa, but it also led to contradictory decisions—such as banning all nuclear weapons from Canada and then buying American Bomarc missiles, which were intended to be armed with nuclear warheads. When Diefenbaker decided to stuff the ends of the missiles with sandbags rather than use nuclear warheads, the Progressive Conservative Party split over the issue. Some agreed with Diefenbaker, while others felt nuclear weapons were needed to adequately protect Canada from Soviet invasion. Some of Diefenbaker's own party members wanted to remove him as leader of the party—which would have meant he would no longer be prime minister.

When Canadians went to the polls in April of 1963, the conflicts in Diefenbaker's Progressive Conservative Party were enough to lose him the election. Lester Pearson of the Liberal Party became Canada's new prime minister, although the Liberals did not win enough seats to form a majority government. Just over half of the seats had been split between the Progressive

President Kennedy meets with pilots from the Cuban reconnaissance mission.

15

*A **free trade agreement** removes restrictions such as tariffs and protective regulations from international trade.*

Conservative Party, the Social Credit Party, and the New Democratic Party (a new party formed in 1961).

Lester Pearson had served as Canadian foreign minister under Prime Minister Louis St. Laurent and had won the Nobel Peace Prize for the creation of United Nations

Canada and the Vietnam War

In the early 1960s, the United States became involved in an unpopular war in Vietnam, fighting with the South Vietnamese against the invading communist forces of North Vietnam. Canada remained officially neutral in the conflict, although Canadians did send relief aid to the South Vietnamese people. When the United States began drafting young men to fight, tens of thousands of them fled to Canada. After the end of the war, some returned to the United States while others chose to stay in Canada.

A low point in Canadian-American relations came during the Vietnam War. Prime Minister Pearson, speaking at Temple University in Philadelphia, Pennsylvania, criticized American actions in Vietnam. American president Lyndon Johnson was furious at Pearson. When they met later, Johnson grabbed Pearson by the front of his shirt and screamed in his face, "You peed on my rug!" Although Pearson was shaken by the encounter, the two men later repaired their friendship.

Lester Pearson

opposition, and he thoroughly disliked Pearson for defeating him in the election. Pearson discovered being prime minister of Canada meant overcoming the obstacles Diefenbaker and the Progressive Conservative Party put in his way.

Despite his minority government and Diefenbaker's opposition, Pearson managed to accomplish a great deal in his five years as prime minister. He improved relations with the United States and helped introduce the Auto Pact, a *free trade agreement* covering the automobile industry. He passed the Medical Care Act in 1968, giving all Canadians a public health-care system, created the Canada Pension Plan to provide for the elderly, and did away with the death penalty in Canada.

The Maple Leaf Flag

Of all Pearson's accomplishments as prime minister, the one he is most remembered for is Canada's flag. Until 1965, Canada's official flag was the Union Jack, Britain's flag, although Canada generally used the Red Ensign, a red flag with the Union Jack in the left hand corner and the shield from Canada's coat of arms. While working with peacekeeping troops in Egypt years before, Pearson realized that Canada needed its

Peacekeeping Forces, which he had proposed at the time of the Suez Crisis in 1956. Despite his successful history, as prime minister with a minority government, Pearson struggled to effectively lead the country. Pearson's campaign slogan had been "60 Days of Decision," but he found this promise difficult to keep during his first months in office. Diefenbaker was now leader of the

Pearson's favorite flag

vored making the Red Ensign Canada's official flag.

When the committee presented their recommendation—the red maple leaf banded by red bars—the House of Commons launched into a series of lengthy, and sometimes heated, debates. Finally, at 2 A.M. on December 15, 1964, the House voted to accept the committee's recommendation. On February 15, 1965, Union Jacks were lowered all across the country, and Canada's new red maple leaf flag was raised for the first time.

Some Canadians disliked the new flag—a few compared it to a Campbell's soup label—but most accepted it readily. With the new flag, Canada took another step away from its British heritage toward developing an identity of its own. The maple leaf had been used as a Canadian symbol since 1700, and including the maple leaf on the Canadian flag celebrated a symbol that was uniquely Canadian.

own flag. The Egyptians had refused to accept Canadian peacekeepers because of the similarity of the British flag to the Canadian flag on the soldiers' uniforms.

In 1964, shortly after becoming prime minister, Pearson announced a call for flag design submissions. He received over two thousand designs, submitted by everyone from artists to schoolchildren. A fifteen-person committee made up of Members of Parliament and Senators from the major political parties met to sort through the design submissions. They presented Pearson with the three designs they had chosen. Pearson's favorite had blue bars on each side and a branch of three red maple leaves in the center. Diefenbaker hated the design and ridiculed it as the "Pearson Pennant." He fa-

The early 1960s were a turbulent time in Canada. Québec had faced explosive changes in the Quiet Revolution and the FLQ had taken advantage of the sense of change to express their own revolutionary views. Canadians, both English- and French-speaking, found a new illustration of their identity in the red maple leaf flag.

The Canadian maple leaf

In the second half of the decade, Canada's growing pains would continue. Canadians, rejoicing in their country, would invite the world to celebrate the centennial with them at Expo 67, and some Québécois would take further steps toward revolutionary *separatism*.

Separatism is the belief that a province should secede from the country.

19

The U.S. Pavilion at Expo 67

Two

A CELEBRATION OF UNITY

People lined up for hours to get into Expo 67, some waiting in line overnight to be one of the first allowed through the gates on opening day. Inside the fairgrounds—built on two Montréal islands in the St. Lawrence River—the gleaming spires and domes of the international pavilions rose, futuristic-looking buildings framed against the sky.

The World's Fair—A Centennial Celebration

After visiting the 1958 World's Fair held in Brussels, Belgium, Canadian senator Mark Drouin returned to Canada brimming with excitement over an idea that had struck him: why not hold the 1967 World's Fair in Canada, in Montréal? In 1967, the country of Canada would be one hundred years old; a World's Fair would be the perfect celebration and a chance to show Canada to the world.

Montréal's mayor liked the idea, and in 1960, the Canadian government submitted an official bid to have the 1967 World's Fair held in Montréal. To the disappointment of Canadians, Canada lost the bid to the Soviet Union. The fair was scheduled to be held in Moscow, where it would be a celebration of the fifty-year anniversary of the USSR. In 1962, however, Moscow changed its mind

about hosting the fair due to the huge cost involved. Canada was instead awarded the bid.

To prepare for Expo 67, construction crews had to expand Île Sainte-Hélène and Île Notre-Dame, making them large enough to house nearly one hundred pavilions, along with an amusement park, aquarium, restaurants, and other buildings. As soon as the construction of the islands themselves was completed, architects and engineers from all over the world descended on Montréal to construct the pavilions.

The work progressed at an amazing speed—all the more impressive since Canada had two fewer years than usual to construct the site. Montréal built a new subway system to bring visitors directly to the fair site from around the city, only the second subway in Canada. At Expo 67, people could ride the minirail above the fairgrounds, take a pedicab (a bicycle-driven taxi), or choose one of the many other means of transportation around the site, including a hovercraft and aerial sky ride.

On April 28, 1967, the first day of Expo 67, over 310,000 people visited the World's Fair, nearly double what the fair committee had estimated. During the six months of the Expo, over five million people would see the exhibitions.

Canadians were very proud of Expo 67.

One Canadian journalist even wrote that the fair was "the greatest thing we have ever done as a nation." People from all over the world visited Montréal and the World's Fair and celebrated the achievement of Canada and the world. The theme of the fair was "Man and His World," and some of the pavilions had names such as "Man the Producer," "Man and Community," "Man the Provider," and "Man the Explorer." Some writers commented enthusiastically that Expo 67 proved the great things French and English Canadians could accomplish when they worked together in harmony.

Canada's Centennial Celebrations took place together with the Expo festivities. Queen Elizabeth II visited, along with

Canada's Expo 67 pavilion

23

many other international guests; the Royal Canadian Mounted Police (RCMP) gave a performance of its Musical Ride; and a massive birthday party on July 1 featured a gigantic birthday cake. The celebrations also included musical and athletic competitions, concerts by Canadian performers, and firework displays and light shows.

Expo 67 from above

*If something is **legitimized**, it has been given legal status.*

A Visit from Charles de Gaulle

One of the many international visitors to Expo 67 was General Charles de Gaulle, president of France and famous World War II hero. The people of Montréal were thrilled at de

Habitat 67

One of the many distinctive buildings at Expo 67 was Habitat. The pile of concrete blocks had been prefabricated and then lifted into place. Habitat was designed by architectural engineering student Moshe Safdie as his master's project. Safdie was dissatisfied with the housing options available to most people. He felt sprawling suburbs took up too much land and were too distant from lively city centers, while urban apartment complexes did not offer families enough space and gave too little privacy and outdoor room. Habitat was intended to give the best of both worlds. Different sized housing units were available, and the roof of one unit became the garden balcony of the unit above it. Initially, Safdie wanted to build 1,000 housing units and intended Habitat to have stores and a school as well. Cost limited the size of the structure to 158 units, however. While visitors to Expo 67 were intrigued by Habitat, few wanted to live there. Safdie had hoped Habitats would spring up all over the world, but no more were ever built. Today, Montréal's Habitat is an exclusive community ten minutes from downtown.

Gaulle's visit and lined the streets cheering as his car passed them. On the evening of July 24, de Gaulle addressed the crowds from the balcony of Montréal's City Hall.

Swelling with emotion, de Gaulle told the

Charles de Gaulle

people of Québec that the festive atmosphere in Montréal as he arrived reminded him of the liberation of France from the occupying Germans during World War II. *"Vive le Québec!"* de Gaulle exclaimed, and the crowd cheered. Long live Québec! *"Vive le Québec . . . ,"* he shouted again, then paused and added, *". . . libre!"* Long live Québec . . . free! The crowd was silent for a moment as people absorbed what de Gaulle had said, and then a great roar of cheers rose into the air.

Some of those listening to de Gaulle's speech were horrified. *"Vive le Québec libre"* was the slogan of the separatist movement, those people who thought Québec should break away from Canada to form its own country. By using the words, the French general had **legitimized** what the separatists were trying to accomplish. The next day, Prime Minister Pearson gave a televised speech, stating that what de Gaulle had said was "unacceptable to Canadians" and that, furthermore, "Canadians do not need to be liberated." In fact, Canadian soldiers had played an important role in the liberation of France at the end of the Second World War. The rest of de Gaulle's visit was cut short, and he returned to France to face criticism from his own government for his speech in Montréal.

Pierre Trudeau

Beginning of the Trudeau Era

At the end of 1967, after Expo 67 had concluded and the centennial celebrations finished, Lester Pearson announced he would be stepping down as prime minister. The news shocked many Canadians, since Pearson was well liked and had served as prime minister for less than five years.

After Pearson's announcement, the Liberal Party began the search for a new party leader. Pierre Trudeau, Pearson's justice minister, was not considered a likely candidate until the top runner dropped out of the race and threw his support behind Trudeau.

Most Canadians did not know much about Trudeau until the Liberal Party leadership convention brought him to their attention. As they saw more of him in the months before the convention, he grew increasingly popular, attracting quite a lot of attention. Trudeau, although at forty-nine was similar in age to many of the other candidates, appeared younger and more stylish than his political contemporaries. A bachelor, he dated actresses and celebrities, wore trendy clothes, and held modern, almost radical, views. As justice minister he had helped get rid of laws making homosexuality illegal and had changed divorce laws, making them more liberal.

On the fourth ballot at the leadership convention, Trudeau was elected Liberal Party leader—and therefore prime minister. Two months later, Canada held a general election, and Canadians overwhelmingly elected Trudeau as prime minister.

Trudeau's popularity continued to grow, blossoming into what became known as Trudeaumania. Crowds of screaming

Pierre Trudeau's famous sense of style

Reviewing First Nations Rights

In 1867, the Canadian government passed the Indian Act, dealing with the First Nations people living on reserves. Many First Nations people were extremely dissatisfied with the Indian Act. They felt many parts of the act were unfair and discriminatory. For example, only those people considered Status Indians could receive the benefits laid out in the Indian Act, but status could easily be lost in a number of ways. In response to requests from First Nations people, Trudeau's minister of Indian affairs, Jean Chrétien, drafted the "Statement of the Canadian Government on Indian Policy," more commonly known as the "White Paper on Indian Affairs." In the introduction, Chrétien wrote, "To be an Indian must be to be free—free to develop Indian cultures in an environment of legal, social and economic equality with other Canadians." While that sounded good, the White Paper appeared to recommend that First Nations be assimilated into Canadian culture, with no special privileges. The First Nations were outraged and banded together to contest the proposals outlined in the White Paper. In 1971, Trudeau withdrew the White Paper, essentially abandoning the ideas it had outlined. In 1985, the Indian Act was finally revised, although many still feel the act has major problems.

teenage girls often greeted the prime minister's appearance in public, and a group of autograph seekers once chased him across the lawn of the Parliament buildings. Many young people admired him intensely. He wore the same types of clothes as they did—including appearing in the House of Commons in sandals—and had a style all his own. The day before the 1968 election, he sat unmoving as a riot broke out at a parade he was attending, with rioting Québec separatists throwing rocks and bottles in his direction. That incident earned him the respect and admiration of many Canadians who had been unsure of him. He was also brilliantly intelligent, with an analytical mind that did not often let emotion get in the way of his goals. Trudeaumania would last until 1971, when Trudeau suddenly married twenty-two-year-old Margaret Sinclair, a woman less than half his age.

Not everyone was thrilled with Trudeau. Many other politicians, including a number in his own party, found him arrogant and far too radical. The New Democratic Party leader, Tommy Douglas, called Trudeau's win in the 1968 election unfair, claiming Trudeau had turned the election into a popularity contest by "kissing young ladies on the lawn."

Official Languages Act

In 1963, after the birth of the FLQ and the increase in Québec separatism, Prime Minister Pearson had instituted the Royal Commission on Bilingualism and Biculturalism. The Royal Commission consisted of a group appointed by the prime minister to study relations between English- and French-speaking Canadians and make recommendations as to how to improve these relations.

In the late 1960s, the Royal Commission turned in its first reports. The problem, the reports stated, was how to bring together a French-speaking majority within Québec and an English-speaking majority in the rest of Canada. The commission recommended making all Canada bilingual, therefore allowing French- and English-speaking Canadians access to information and services in their own language no matter where in Canada they happened to live.

Trudeau agreed with the commission's suggestion. He believed Canada needed both French and English as its official languages and that such a bilingualism could only make the country stronger. Confining French to Québec only led to the province's isolation from the rest of Canada and feelings of inequality. Such a "them and us"

Canadian traffic signs appear in both official languages.

attitude could not continue if Canada was to survive united.

In 1968, Trudeau proposed the Official Languages Act. Introducing the bill in the House of Commons, he spoke to the assembled Members of Parliament:

> French Canada can survive not by turning in on itself but by reaching out to claim its full share of every aspect of Canadian life. English Canada should not attempt to crush or expect to absorb French Canada. All Canadians should capitalize on the advantages of living in a country which has learned to speak in two great world languages.

In 1969, the Official Languages Act went into effect. The act acknowledged both French and English as Canada's official languages and ensured federal services would be provided in both languages. Some English-speaking Canadians worried they would be forced to speak French, but the purpose of the act was only to guarantee everyone would be able to find federal help in their own language.

The late 1960s had been an exhilarating time for Canadians. Expo 67 had been a high point for many, attracting celebrities from around the world and revealing Canada as an important member of the international community. The election of Pierre Trudeau in 1968 only helped contribute to Canada's new fashionable image.

Québec's separatism had not ended with the Official Languages Act, however. In 1970, the FLQ would reemerge, forcing Prime Minister Trudeau to take strong measures to stop them.

Troops deployed to Québec during the October crisis

Three
CRISIS IN QUÉBEC

On Monday, October 5, 1970, at 8:15 in the morning, British trade commissioner James Cross left his Montréal home to go to work as usual. Suddenly, as his horrified wife looked on, four armed men leaped out and forced Cross into a waiting taxi. At first, no one knew who was behind the kidnapping, or what had motivated it. Then, in the afternoon, ransom notes were delivered, identifying the kidnappers as the Liberation cell of the FLQ and listing numerous demands in exchange for Cross's release. The demands included $500,000 in gold, an airplane to transport the kidnappers to Cuba, and the release of twenty-three prisoners. The kidnappers also wanted the FLQ manifesto to be read aloud in the national media.

The FLQ Crisis

The FLQ had not been completely inactive since the bombings and arrests of 1963. They had continued to carry out armed robberies and bombings from time to time, but Canadians generally considered them a background irritation rather than a major threat. The kidnapping of James Cross in October of 1970 shocked Canadians; suddenly the FLQ seemed like much more of a danger.

Most Canadians thought the FLQ's demands were ridiculous; the only one initially met was the reading of the manifesto on a few radio stations. On October 10, Jérôme Choquette, Québec's minister of justice, tried to compromise with the kidnappers, offering them safe passage out of Canada but refusing to release the twenty-three prisoners.

At seven o'clock on the evening Choquette issued his offer to the FLQ, Québec's minister of labour Pierre Laporte was tossing a football back and forth with his nephew on the front lawn of his home when a car pulled up to the curb and two masked men leaped out, armed with machine guns. The men grabbed Laporte and forced him into the car. Laporte's nephew ran to the car and tried to see in, but the car sped off.

Pierre Laporte

The Laporte kidnapping frightened Canadians even more than the Cross kidnapping had; now they knew the first had not been an isolated incident. Laporte had been abducted by a different cell of the FLQ. From their communications, the Chénier cell

The War Measures Act made headlines.

appeared to be much more radical and violent than the Liberation cell, which had taken Cross.

Some believed the Canadian government should give in to the kidnappers to save the lives of the hostages, but Trudeau disagreed, along with most Canadians. At a press conference on October 13, he responded to questions about what his response would be to the kidnappings: "I think the society must take every means at its disposal to defend itself against the emergence of a parallel power which defies the elected power in this country and I think that this goes to any distance."

On October 15, Robert Bourassa, Québec's premier, asked Trudeau to impose the War Measures Act. The War Measures Act had been passed at the beginning of World War I and gave the prime minister and his cabinet the power to act without consulting Parliament. Under the act, Trudeau could deal with events quickly as they arose, without having to go through the sometimes-lengthy process of gaining Parliamentary approval for each action. The House of Commons agreed with the decision to pass the War Measures Act, and it took effect on the same day, October 15. Trudeau was concerned about the effect the act might have on the hostages, but felt he

Robert Bourassa when he was Quebec's premier

could not allow a terrorist group to control the government's actions.

The War Measures Act allowed the army to patrol the streets, freeing police to focus on finding a way to rescue the hostages and the search for FLQ members. Over 250 people were arrested during the next two days, people suspected of being associated with the FLQ or who had supported them in some way. The police hoped to apprehend some of the key FLQ members with this sweep, although almost all those arrested were eventually released without being charged.

In response to the arrests, the Liberation cell of the FLQ, holding James Cross, issued a statement on October 17 in which they claimed—contrary to past statements—to have no intention of killing Cross. Only if the police found them and raided their hiding place would Cross be killed. The statement also said the Chénier cell was considering what should be done with Pierre Laporte. Police believed the two cells were not in communication with each other and

The Multicultural Act

In 1971, Prime Minister Trudeau passed the Multicultural Act. Although immigrants from many world cultures already lived throughout Canada, this act celebrated Canada's multicultural nature. The most important point of the Multicultural Act was to ensure all Canadians had equal rights, no matter their background. In the early twentieth century, the majority of immigrants arriving in Canada had been from European backgrounds. From the 1970s on, though, most immigrants came from non-European heritages.

Task Force on Canadian Unity

The election of a separatist government in Québec alarmed the federal government. In response, Trudeau appointed the Task Force on Canadian Unity. The purpose of the task force was to talk to Canadians and find out their opinions on how unified Canada was, then to make recommendations on how to better unite the country. After their first meeting in 1977, the task force published a preliminary statement:

The Task Force . . . recognizes that Canada and its present federal system are under great stress. The creation of the Task Force is itself a testimony to this. All regions of Canada are reflecting and expressing this malaise. The most pressing questions are being raised in Quebec and the Task Force intends to give these high priority. Nevertheless, the concerns of other regions are vitally important and will be given our full attention.

When the task force submitted its report in 1979, they recommended more power be given to the provincial governments. While Trudeau and the federal government spent a lot of time studying the findings of the task force, they mostly ignored the recommendations in the drafting of the 1982 Canadian constitution.

that this was how the members of the Liberation cell hoped to influence the Chénier cell not to kill Laporte.

Whether or not the Chénier cell would have followed the example of the Liberation cell will never be known. On the same day as the Liberation cell issued their statement, someone called a Montréal radio station claiming Laporte had been killed. Later calls to the same station directed police to a nearby airfield, where Laporte's body was discovered in the trunk of a car. Years later, an investigation into the murder revealed that Laporte might have been killed by accident, strangled by mistake in an effort to keep him quiet.

After the murder of Laporte, nothing seemed to happen for a while. In early November, police discovered and raided the hiding place of the Chénier cell, although most of the members were able to escape and only one was arrested. Finally, in early December, police discovered the location of the Liberation cell, and on December 3, they freed James Cross from his eight weeks of captivity.

The members of the Liberation cell were all *exiled* to Cuba and not allowed to return to Canada on pain of arrest. The

*Someone who is **exiled** has been forced to leave his country.*

Terrorism shattered the peace of Montréal, Québec's capital city.

Un parti propre au Québec

BLOC QUÉBÉCOIS

The Parti Québécois's logo

remaining members of the Chénier cell were arrested on December 28 and charged with kidnapping and murder.

Before the kidnappings of James Cross and Pierre Laporte, some Québec separatists had begun to think violence might be the way to get their views heard by the federal government and the rest of Canada. After the FLQ crisis, violence did not look like such a good idea. The FLQ had not succeeded in their attempts to begin a revolution in Québec and instead had united the country against them. Canadians, including those in Québec, overwhelmingly approved of Trudeau's War Measures Act, believing the step had been necessary to break the terrorist organization. After 1970, Québec separatists would turn to politics rather than terrorism.

René Lévesque

Parti Québécois

During the early and mid-1960s, René Lévesque had been an active member of the Québec Liberal Party, serving as minister of

natural resources in the Québec provincial cabinet. In 1967, Lévesque left the Liberal Party because of his frustration over the party's refusal to discuss the question of *sovereignty* for Québec. The next year, he formed the Parti Québécois (PQ), a merger of several smaller separatist groups.

While attracting the attention of the Québécois, the PQ gained only a few seats in the Québec Parliament during the early 1970s. Then, in 1976, the PQ swept the election, gaining 71 of 110 seats, and Réne Lévesque became Québec's premier.

Sovereignty means self-government.

Turning from the violence of the FLQ, the Québec people had chosen a separatist party to lead them.

In 1974, Québec premier Robert Bourassa had passed Bill 22, making French the only official language in Québec. Although Canada was a bilingual country, most provinces were unilingual, with English as the only official language. In 1977, Lévesque and the PQ government went a step further and passed Bill 101, the Charter of the French Language. Bill 101 outlawed English on signs and made it more difficult for English-speaking people in Québec to have access to education in their own language. The French still worried their distinct language and culture could be overwhelmed by the English language and culture predominant in Canada. Bill 101 was intended to prevent that possibility.

Referendum on Québec

In 1980, René Lévesque and the PQ decided to hold a *referendum* to determine how the

Québec City

*A **referendum** is a vote by the whole electorate on a specific question or questions put to it by a government.*

45

people of Québec felt about actually separating from the rest of Canada and forming their own country. The question put to voters at the May 20 referendum was:

> The Government of Quebec has made public its proposal to negotiate a new agreement with the rest of Canada, based on the equality of nations; this agreement would enable Quebec to acquire the exclusive power to make its laws, levy its taxes and establish relations abroad—in other words, sovereignty—and at the same time to maintain with Canada an economic association including a common currency; any change in political status resulting from these negotiations will be effected with approval by the people through another referendum; on these terms, do you give the Government of Quebec the mandate to negotiate the proposed agreement between Quebec and Canada?

In other words, the referendum was asking to enter into talks with the Canadian government that could lead to Québec becoming a separate country—although one closely linked to Canada through economic ties.

While Lévesque campaigned for the "yes" side of the issue, Prime Minister Trudeau led the campaign for the "no" side. Canadians watched anxiously to learn the outcome of the vote, and more than one hundred Montréal-based businesses moved their corporate headquarters to Toronto, fearing they might suddenly find themselves operating outside Canada.

The voter turnout was large, over 85 percent; this was an issue in which the people of Québec were very interested, whichever way they intended to vote. When the results were in, no one was really surprised, although many were relieved; the "no" side had won, with 60 percent of the votes—Québec would not be leaving Canada. Bill 22 and Bill 101 had satisfied many who might otherwise have been tempted to vote for separation.

Lévesque was disappointed, but he concluded the time was not yet right for Québec sovereignty. "If I've understood you well," he said in his concession speech, "you're telling me 'until next time.'" On the other hand, Trudeau, while pleased with the victory, was concerned with the 40 percent who had voted for separation. At a press conference he spoke to the people of Québec, promising them changes would come. At the time, Trudeau and the provincial premiers were in the middle of talks regarding constitutional reform. Trudeau promised he and the premiers would work to make all Canadians, including those in Québec, proud to live in Canada.

The 1970s were a tumultuous time for Québec. From the FLQ crisis of 1970 to the Québec Referendum of 1980, Québec had gone through considerable growing pains in the span of a decade.

The 1960s and 1970s had also been a time of growing environmental awareness throughout Canada. New technologies and power sources created concerns among many that the environment could be permanently damaged. New groups were formed to address these concerns.

Québec emerged from its growing pains as a prosperous modern province.

47

Canadians know the importance of caring for their environment.

Four
ENVIRONMENTAL CONCERNS

In October of 1969, the United States conducted a nuclear test on Amchitka Island, one of the Aleutian Islands in Alaska. A group of concerned environmentalists from Vancouver, British Columbia, horrified at the ecological damage the testing could cause, formed the "Don't Make a Wave Committee," named for the tidal wave the test had triggered. Two years later, on September 15, 1971, the group left Vancouver in a boat named *Greenpeace*. They intended to protest against another nuclear test set to be carried out on the same island. The U.S. Coast Guard stopped the boat 600 miles (965 kilometers) from their goal, but they had succeeded in raising awareness for their cause and environmental issues in general. People from across Canada, and in the United States as well, launched a string of environmental protests. Although the U.S. government continued with the planned test, it soon ended the testing program in Alaska. After the voyage of the *Greenpeace*, the Greenpeace Foundation was created in Vancouver, British Columbia, to continue to actively protect the earth's natural environment.

Activism is vigorous and sometimes aggressive action in pursuit of a political or social goal.

Idealism is aspiring to or living in accordance with high standards or principles.

The **hippie movement** was a 1960s phenomenon composed of young people who rejected accepted social and political values and professed to believe in universal peace and love.

The **feminist movement** was an organized attempt to gain equal rights and equal opportunities for women.

A New Awareness

For centuries, Canadians believed their natural resources were inexhaustible. Since Canada had so many large, uninhabited wilderness areas, people thought human actions could never be great enough to affect the environment. During the 1960s and '70s, this perception began to change. People became aware that the environment was important, not just for its beauty, but also because what happened in nature affected the human population. Many Canadians became concerned about the increasing pollution problems created by growing populations and by chemicals released into the air and water by factories and new energy sources. More people understood the importance of conservation, the need to protect endangered species so they would not become extinct while preserving natural resources.

The creation of the Greenpeace Foundation in 1971 was a sign of this increased environmental awareness. The 1960s were a time of *activism*; the baby boom generation was growing up with a strong sense of *idealism* and a desire to change the world. Out of this desire for change grew such diverse movements as the *hippie movement*, the *feminist movement*, and the environmental movement. People wanted to make the world a better place for future generations.

The harp seal is just one of Canada's endangered species.

51

Mushroom cloud from an atomic bomb

In 1971, Environment Canada was established, a government group headed by the minister of the environment. Environment Canada had the same general goals as organizations such as Greenpeace—to protect natural resources and work toward environmentally friendly laws.

The demand for energy had grown in the twentieth century, prompting concerns among many environmentalists. More people owned automobiles, creating a large demand for the oil used to make gasoline. The discovery of nuclear energy in the 1940s had caused scientists to study how the power of atomic *fission* could be harnessed as an energy supply—but the use of nuclear power alarmed many, who feared accidents at nuclear power plants could lead to horrific catastrophes rivaling the destruction caused by the atomic bombs dropped on Hiroshima and Nagasaki, Japan, at the end of World War II.

Fission is the induced splitting of an atom nucleus into smaller nuclei, usually accompanied by a significant release of energy.

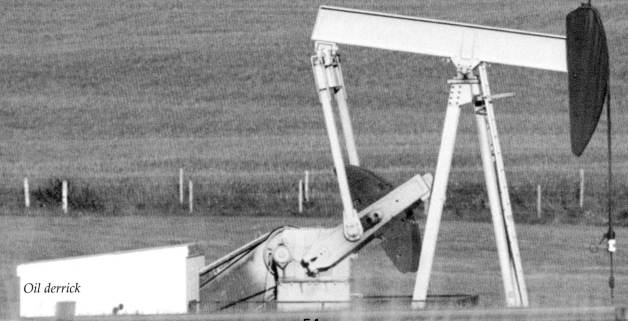

Oil derrick

The Oil Boom

In the mid-1940s, the Imperial Oil Company drilled over one hundred holes across Alberta and Saskatchewan, looking for oil and finding none. Then, in February 1947, the company drilled a hole in Leduc, Alberta, fifty miles (80 kilometers) from any other test holes. Imperial Oil did not expect to find oil in Leduc, but it was running low on oil reserves and desperately needed to find a new source. The company drilled in Leduc because it was willing to look anywhere. When the hole was wet rather than dry, they were ecstatic. By the end of the year, the company had drilled 147 more oil wells in the area. The size of the oil field was greater than the company could have anticipated.

Until the discovery of the Leduc oil field, agriculture had been the main industry in Alberta. With the new discovery, oil production and refining quickly became the largest industry in Alberta, bringing increased wealth to the province. When the world experienced an oil crisis in 1973, brought on by conflicts in the Middle Eastern oil-producing countries, Alberta grew extremely rich since it had oil to offer.

The oil industry created concerns among environmentalists and conservationists as environmental awareness grew and oil production continued to rise. Environmental groups worried about the effect the drilling was having or could have on natural resources. Among the concerns was the threat of oil spills, in which large amounts of oil could contaminate water or land, killing

Offshore Oil and the Ocean Ranger

The quest for new oil fields continued to grow and oil companies began searching the ocean floor for new sources of fuel. To drill under water, large oil platforms were needed. This brought engineering challenges, as well as environmental ones. Drilling platforms needed to be strong enough to withstand the wind and storms found on the open seas. The dangers of an oil spill were also greater with offshore drilling. In 1980, the Ocean Ranger, a semi-submersible drilling platform, began operation on the Grand Banks, off the coast of Newfoundland. At the time, the Ocean Ranger was the largest platform of its kind in the world. People believed the platform was indestructible, since it was so large. Then, on February 14, 1982, a large wave struck the platform during a storm. Soon, another wave struck, shorting out the control panel. The wave had also thrown the platform off balance. When the men tried to pump the water out of the lower side of the rig, they accidentally pumped more water in. Soon, the Ocean Ranger had tipped completely and begun sinking. All 84 men aboard the platform drowned in the icy Atlantic waters. The Ocean Ranger disaster inspired stricter safety regulations in offshore drilling.

thousands of birds, fish, and animals. In January 1973, the oil tanker *Irish Stardust* ran aground near the north end of Vancouver Island, spilling almost 100,000 gallons (378,000 liters) of oil onto British Columbia's beaches. This spill proved the danger of oil contamination.

Nuclear Energy

In the early twentieth century, scientists all over the world studied the structure of the atom. In 1945, this research led to the first atomic bombs being dropped on Japan at the end of World War II. After the war,

Nuclear plant

57

CANDU Reactors vs. Traditional Reactors

CANDU reactors are a special type of nuclear reactor developed by Canada. CANDU reactors are also sometimes called pressurized heavy-water reactors. Key differences between pressurized heavy-water reactors and light-water reactors (the traditional American design) are the use of natural uranium, the use of pressure tubes to hold fuel, and the use of heavy water. The alternative to using pressure tubes is the use of a single large pressure vessel. The separate pressure tubes allow the fuel to be replaced without stopping reactor operation, significantly reducing downtime. Heavy water absorbs neutrons at a lower rate than normal (light) water does. This allows the use of natural uranium, which does not have as much fissionable material as enriched uranium. (Fissionable material is what is used to create the nuclear reaction.) This in turn eliminates the expensive and time-consuming step of enriching uranium.

American scientists developed nuclear reactors, whose whole purpose was to produce material for nuclear weapons. In the 1950s, reactors began to be built to provide electricity instead of weapons.

In Canada, the first nuclear-generated power was produced in 1962 at the Nuclear Power Demonstration (NPD) Reactor near Rolphton, Ontario. The NPD Reactor was an early version of the Canadian-developed

Canadian logging practices came under fire from environmentalists.

Factory pollution

CANDU (CANada Deuterium Uranium) reactor. The CANDU reactor ran on *heavy water*, making it cheaper to run than traditional reactors. During the 1970s, Canada sold a number of these CANDU reactors to developing countries, who could more easily afford this type of reactor. Critics worried, however, that the nuclear processes in CANDU reactors could make it easier for these countries to develop nuclear weapons than they would be able to do with more traditional reactors.

As Canada and other countries built more nuclear reactors as power plants, environmentalists became increasingly alarmed. Many environmental groups felt there was no such thing as safe nuclear power. The chance always existed of accidental radiation leaks, and the use of such reactors always left barrels of radioactive waste as by-products, which needed to be disposed.

New technologies and power sources brought new environmental threats to be confronted. Activist groups, such as Greenpeace, campaigned to raise awareness of dangers facing the natural world, often taking extreme measures to stop the spread of environmental threats. Such measures often included Greenpeace members attempting to use their bodies to stop the continuation of the practice they were campaigning against, for example by lying in front of construction equipment to stop the building of a new nuclear power plant or by chaining themselves to trees to stop loggers from cutting them down.

Environment Canada, on the other hand, while working toward the same goal of protecting the environment, used government channels to pass laws leading to stricter safety standards for nuclear reactors and laws protecting the natural environment. Even before the founding of Environment

Heavy water is water that has had its hydrogen atoms replaced with deuterium, a hydrogen isotope.

The logging industry faced growing controversy.

Canada in 1971, the federal government had worked to pass environmental laws, such as banning phosphates in laundry detergents,

Air and water pollution are growing concerns for Canadians.

which left a constant sudsy residue in rivers and lakes. Factories found releasing pollutants into the air were fined severely. In 1972, fishing was banned off certain coasts due to declining numbers of fish.

The environment would remain an ongoing concern throughout the twentieth century and into the twenty-first, as government and industry tried to balance efficiency with ecological responsibility. Groups like Greenpeace and government organizations such as Environment Canada played roles in trying to keep Canada environmentally healthy. While Greenpeace raised awareness through gaining media publicity, Environment Canada worked with lawmakers to pass stricter regulations to protect the natural world.

The early 1980s would bring the Trudeau era to a close, but first the prime minister would succeed in passing the Constitution Act. In 1982, Canada would finally become completely independent from Britain.

ELIZABETH THE SECOND

By the grace of God of the United Kingdom, Canada and her other Realms and Territories Queen, Head of the Commonwealth, defender of the faith.

To all to whom these presents shall come or whom the same may in anyway concern,

GREETING:

A PROCLAMATION

Attorney General of Canada

Elizabeth R

WHEREAS in the past certain amendments to the Constitution of Canada have been made by the Parliament of the United Kingdom at the request and with the consent of Canada;

AND WHEREAS it is in accord with the status of Canada as an independent state that Canadians be able to amend their Constitution in Canada in all respects;

AND WHEREAS it is desirable to provide in the Constitution of Canada for the recognition of certain fundamental rights and freedoms and to make other amendments to the Constitution;

AND WHEREAS the Parliament of the United Kingdom has therefore, at the request and with the consent of Canada, enacted the Canada Act, which provides for the patriation and amendment of the Constitution of Canada;

AND WHEREAS Section 58 of the Constitution Act, 1982, set out in Schedule B to the Canada Act, provides that the Constitution Act, 1982 shall, subject to section 59 thereof come into force on a day to be fixed by proclamation issued under the Great Seal of Canada;

NOW KNOW You that We, by and with the advice of Our Privy Council for Canada, do by this Our Proclamation, declare that the Constitution Act, 1982 shall, subject to section 59 thereof, come into force on the Seventeenth day of April, in the year of Our Lord One Thousand Nine Hundred and Eighty-two.

ALL WHICH Our Loving Subjects and all others whom these Presents may concern are hereby required to take notice and to govern themselves accordingly.

IN TESTIMONY WHEREOF We have caused these Our Letters to be made Patent and the Great Seal of Canada to be hereunto affixed. At Our City of Ottawa, this Seventeenth day of April in the Year of Our Lord One Thousand Nine Hundred and Eighty-two and in the Thirty-first Year of Our Reign.

By Her Majesty's Command

Registrar General of Canada

Prime Minister of Canada

GOD SAVE THE QUEEN

ELIZABETH DEU

PAR LA GRÂCE de dieu reine du Ro Canada et de ses autres royaum chef du commonwealth, défense

À tous ceux que les présentes pe manière concerner,

SALUT:

PROCLAMATION

Le procureur général du Canada

CONSIDÉRANT qu'à la demande et avec le consentement du Canada, le Parleme Uni a déjà modifié à plusieurs reprises la Constitution du Can

qu'en vertu de leur appartenance à un État souverain, les Canadiens se tout pouvoir de modifier leur Constitution au Canada;

qu'il est souhaitable d'inscrire dans la Constitution du Canada la recom certain nombre de libertés et de droits fondamentaux et d'y apporter d'aut

QUE le Parlement du Royaume-Uni, à la demande et avec le consentement adopté en conséquence, la Loi sur le Canada, qui prévoit le rapatriement de canadienne et sa modification;

QUE l'article 58, figurant à l'annexe B de la Loi sur le Canada, stipule que, se l'article 59, la Loi constitutionnelle de 1982 entrera en vigueur à une d proclamation sous le grand sceau du Canada;

NOUS PROCLAMONS, sur l'avis de Notre Conseil privé pour le Canada, qu constitutionnelle de 1982 entrera en vigueur; sous réserve de l'article 59, le jour du mois d'avril en l'an de grâce mil neuf cent quatre-vingt-deux.

NOUS DEMANDONS À Nos loyaux sujets et à toute autre personne concer acte de la présente proclamation.

EN FOI DE QUOI, Nous avons rendu les présentes lettres patentes et y avons grand sceau du Canada.

Fait en Notre ville d'Ottawa, ce dix-septième jour du mois d'avril en l'an neuf cent quatre-vingt-deux, le trente et unième de Notre règne.

Par ordre de Sa Majesté

Le registraire général du Canada

Le premier ministre du Canada

DIEU PROTÈGE LA REINE

Five
CANADA'S NEW CONSTITUTION

In 1867, the British North America Act had created the country of Canada, independent from Great Britain. Nevertheless, Canada was still closely tied with Britain. When Britain entered World War I in 1914, it requested Canada send soldiers to help. The Canadian prime minister, speaking to Canadians, confirmed that the only possible response was, "Ready, aye. Ready!"

Until the Statute of Westminster in 1931, Canada did not legally hold the same status as Britain. Canada was a member of the British Empire, *subordinate* to Britain in international affairs. The Statute of Westminster officially gave Canada international independence.

In the early 1980s, however, Canada still did not have the power to make changes to its constitution. At several times earlier in the twentieth century, the Canadian government had tried to bring about constitutional reform, which would allow Canada to have complete power to make changes in its

Subordinate means secondary in importance.

own constitution. However, all the provincial premiers needed to agree on the new constitution, and no one could work out an agreement as to the details of how amendments would be made to the constitution.

Fighting for Canada's Constitution

In 1980, Prime Minister Trudeau told Canadians he was determined to give the country a new constitution. So determined

Queen Elizabeth signing the new constitution

Trudeau's victory dance after Queen Elizabeth signed the Canada Act

was he, in fact, that, while he would try to seek agreement among the provincial premiers, he claimed that if he could not reach such an agreement, he would take matters into his own hands and bring in a new constitution himself. Many Members of Parliament were horrified at this idea, although the Supreme Court of Canada eventually declared a unanimous decision was not necessary, but only a general consensus.

Throughout 1981, the premiers battled back and forth. In April, eight premiers—those from all provinces except Ontario and New Brunswick—met and worked out a constitutional agreement of their own. Trudeau rejected their version of a new constitution, since they had left out a Charter of Rights and Freedoms, and because they had given more power to the provinces than the federal government. Trudeau strongly favored federalism, a strong central government, rather than giving the individual provinces extensive freedoms to act on their own.

One problem Trudeau faced was the Parti Québécois and René Lévesque, who, as leaders of a separatist government, could not agree to strengthen the federal government of Canada. Lévesque believed Québec would be better off governing itself, without the rest of Canada. Agreeing to a new constitution giving more power to the federal government would have gone against everything he believed.

In early November 1981, the premiers met again. For days, they argued, apparently getting nowhere. Trudeau was almost ready to give up again, until November 4. While the prime minister and the premiers met in a conference room, three men met in the kitchen next door—Justice Minister Jean Chrétien, Ontario attorney general Roy McMurtry, and Saskatchewan attorney general Roy Romanow. These men spent the morning going over the various constitutional proposals and sketching out their own proposal. They pulled together the points on which most had agreed and decided which points could be compromised. Then they began approaching the premiers individually. Throughout the rest of the day and into the night, the men slowly convinced other premiers, who in turn convinced others. Meanwhile, Québec's premier Lévesque had gone to bed, unaware of the discussions going on secretly around him. By early morning, the agreement of all the premiers but Lévesque had been gained, and Trudeau had agreed to the compromises as well. Lévesque was presented with the new proposal in the morning, but he refused to have anything to do with it.

Lévesque swore he would never sign the new constitution and claimed that once again Québec had been left alone while the rest of Canada banded together against it. In reality, it was the separatists who had been left alone. Prime Minister Trudeau was himself from Québec, as was Justice Minister Jean Chrétien, who had helped to draft the final constitutional proposal. Many of the Members of Parliament who eventually voted to approve the new constitution were also from Québec, although few were from the Parti Québécois.

Charter of Rights and Freedoms

Trudeau made sure the new constitution included a Charter of Rights and Freedoms. The charter began:

Whereas Canada is founded upon principles that recognize the supremacy of God and the rule of law:

Guarantee of Rights and Freedoms

1. The Canadian Charter of Rights and Freedoms guarantees the rights and freedoms set out in it subject only to such reasonable limits prescribed by law as can be demonstrably justified in a free and democratic society.

Fundamental Freedoms

2. Everyone has the following fundamental freedoms:
    a) freedom of conscience and religion;
    b) freedom of thought, belief, opinion and expression, including freedom of the press and other media of communication;
    c) freedom of peaceful assembly; and
    d) freedom of association.

The final proposal included the formula for constitutional amendments put forward by the eight premiers in April and also included Trudeau's Charter of Rights and Freedoms, although with some changes. The major change involving the Charter of Rights and Freedoms was the notwithstanding clause. This allowed the provinces to choose not to follow certain parts of the charter, simply by invoking the notwithstanding clause. The clause was intended to satisfy those premiers who felt their provincial rights could be overrun by the new constitution. One of the points Lévesque had wanted to include was a *veto power* for Québec on constitutional questions, but this was not included in the final version. Québec would, however, make extensive use of the notwithstanding clause.

Veto power is the ability of one branch of government to reject the legislation of another.

The Canada Act

Once Prime Minister Trudeau and the majority of the provincial premiers had agreed on the form of the new constitution, Britain still had to agree. The Canadian government requested the British Parliament pass an act proclaiming the new Canadian constitution as law.

British Parliament responded by drafting the Canada Act, and on March 29, 1982, Queen Elizabeth II gave her royal assent to the act. One last step needed to be taken before Canada had its new constitution, however. At a ceremony in Ottawa on April 17, 1982, the Queen signed the Canada Act. At that moment, Canada had its new constitution. From that point on, Canada could make its own constitutional changes without petitioning Britain to pass constitutional laws for it. Thousands of Canadians attended the outdoor ceremony,

Pierre Trudeau

braving rain and chilly weather to watch history being made. As the Queen signed the document, a band began to play, and the crowds cheered, waving tiny Canadian flags. Back in Québec, Premier Lévesque ordered all the provincial flags be lowered to half mast.

The End of the Trudeau Era

The Canadian Constitution of 1982 had been a high point of Trudeau's career. He had tried for over a decade to give Canada a new constitution, one that would free it from having to approach Britain to accomplish constitutional changes. Still, he had isolated Québec in the final draft of the constitution. By 2005, Québec still had not signed the constitution, although this did not mean the constitution did not apply in that province. Rather, by withholding their signatures, Québec premiers have made a symbolic protest over the way they felt the constitution treated their province. To satisfy them, changes would have to be made affirming Québec's distinct language and culture and giving Québec veto power on constitutional questions.

The two years after the introduction of the Canadian constitution marked a major decline in Trudeau's popularity. Unemployment began to rise without a corresponding drop in inflation. Canada's national debt was also huge, having leaped 1,200 percent during the Trudeau years.

Late in February of 1984, Trudeau went for what he described as "a long walk in the snow." When he returned, he announced he would be stepping down as prime minister. In the months before, the media had talked about the tide of public opinion that was turning against Trudeau. Trudeaumania was definitely a thing of the past. Trudeau himself, in an interview later in his life, acknowledged the oddity of Trudeaumania. He had never expected it to last, he admitted, since it had been based on emotion rather than a true agreement with his political beliefs. And, once he was married, many of the young girls, who made up a large component of those infected with Trudeaumania, did not find him nearly as attractive. Trudeau faced public humiliation when his marriage broke up.

On June 30, 1984, Pierre Trudeau resigned, and John Turner became interim prime minister. Turner would not last long as prime minister, losing the general election to Brian Mulroney and the Political Conservative Party less than three months later.

Despite the fact that some had actively hated Trudeau at the time of his resignation, Canadians remained fascinated with the man. He was often rude and could be vulgar. He was arrogant and did not seem to care what people thought of him. Nevertheless, he did everything with style, from sliding down banisters to the trademark red rose he wore in his lapel.

Years after he had stepped down as

Trudeau and the Western Provinces

In his final years as prime minister, Trudeau alienated many Western Canadians. They felt he did not understand the issues they faced and that he was not sympathetic with their problems. In 1980, Trudeau instituted the National Energy Policy, as a response to the energy crisis of the 1970s. The National Energy Policy promoted the search for alternate energy sources, further oil drilling to find new oil fields in Canada, and higher taxes on oil production, which would lead to higher revenues for the federal government. Oil-producing Alberta despised the National Energy Policy. Farmers in the prairies had no reason to love Trudeau either, after he casually dismissed their grievances. "A farmer is a complainer," he said with a shrug. Only years after Trudeau's resignation did Western Canadians finally admit to a grudging respect of the former prime minister.

prime minister, many of those who had disliked him had come to admire him. In a poll taken in January of 2000, Canadians ranked Trudeau as the top prime minister of the century, gaining 41 percent of the votes. When he died of prostate cancer in September of 2000 (having hidden the disease from the public until his death), thousands turned out to pay their respects at his funeral in Montréal. In 2004, another survey ranked him number three on a list of the greatest Canadians in history.

Trudeau brought out strong feelings in people. Whether they loved him or hated him, he above all fascinated them. Anyone who had lived through his sixteen years as prime minister would never forget him.

The nearly a quarter of century between 1960 and 1984 had been a time of often

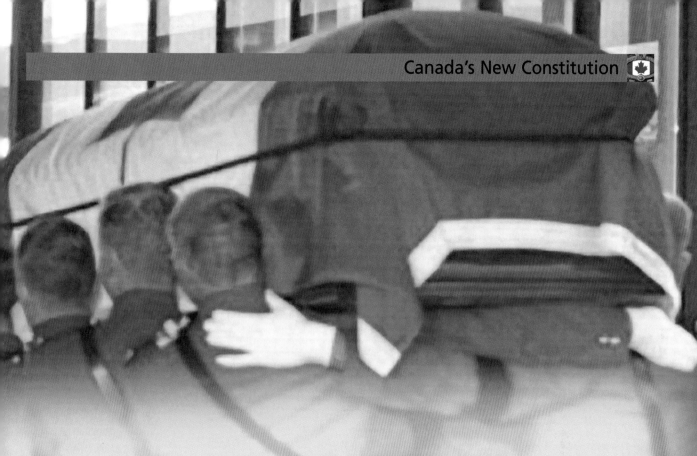

Trudeau's funeral

painful changes in Canada. The Quiet Revolution in Québec set off changes in the province that Jean Lesage, who had initiated the reforms, could never have foreseen. The people of Québec worried about their language and culture being absorbed by the rest of Canada. This fear inspired the FLQ, the terrorist organization responsible for bombings, robberies, and kidnappings in Montréal. The same emotions that had pro-duced the FLQ also produced the Parti Québécois, a separatist political party that would gain leadership of the province in the mid-1970s.

While Québec struggled to maintain its unique society, Canada as a whole struggled with a sort of identity crisis. What did it mean to be Canadian? Values embraced during the 1960s and '70s included multiculturalism and a commitment to the environment. In 1965, Canada had adopted its new flag, giving Canadians a symbol to claim as their own. In 1969, the Official Languages Act gave English and French equal status at the federal level. To be Canadian meant respecting all people, even those who disagreed with you—so Justin Trudeau declared in his eulogy for his father, the former prime minister.

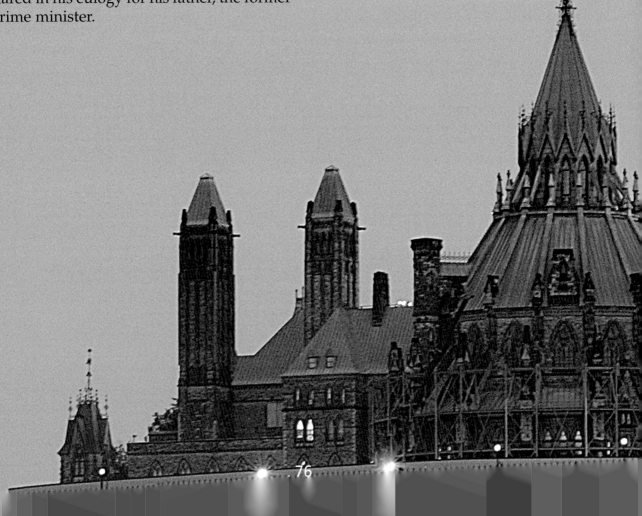

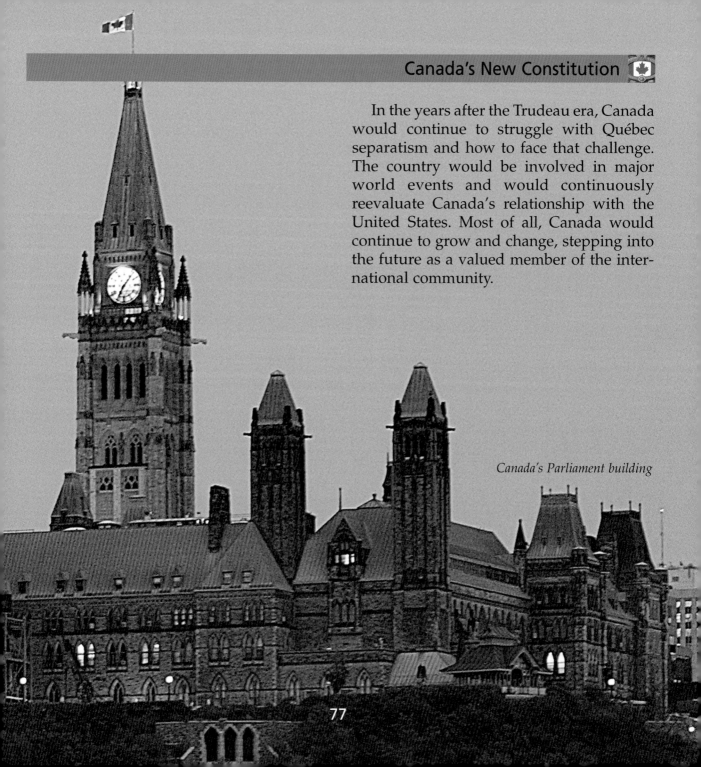

In the years after the Trudeau era, Canada would continue to struggle with Québec separatism and how to face that challenge. The country would be involved in major world events and would continuously reevaluate Canada's relationship with the United States. Most of all, Canada would continue to grow and change, stepping into the future as a valued member of the international community.

Canada's Parliament building

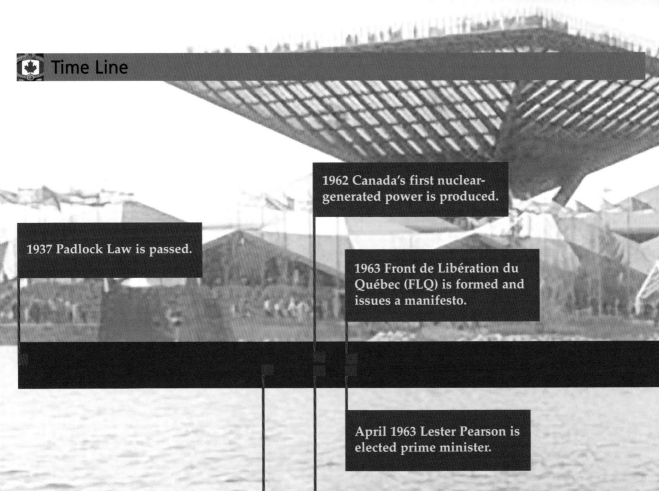

1962 Canada's first nuclear-generated power is produced.

1937 Padlock Law is passed.

1963 Front de Libération du Québec (FLQ) is formed and issues a manifesto.

April 1963 Lester Pearson is elected prime minister.

October 1962 Cuban Missile Crisis occurs between the United States and the Soviet Union.

June 22 1960 Québec Liberal Party takes control of Canadian Parliament.

1968 Medical Care Act is passed, providing health care to all Canadians.

February 15, 1965 The red maple leaf flag is raised as the national flag for the first time.

October 1969 The United States conducts a nuclear test on Amchitka Island.

1967 World's Fair is held in Montréal.

1968 Pierre Trudeau elected prime minister.

1968 Prime Minister Trudeau introduces the Official Languages Act to Parliament; the act goes into effect in 1969.

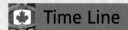

October 15, 1970 Pierre Trudeau imposes the War Measures Act.

October 5, 1970 James Cross is kidnapped by a branch of the FLQ; he is freed December 3.

1971 Environment Canada is established.

1971 Greenpeace Foundation is formed.

October 10, 1970 Another branch of the FLQ kidnaps Québec minister of labor Pierre Laporte; he is later found murdered.

1980 Québec Parliament holds a referendum on secession; it fails.

June 30, 1984 Pierre Trudeau resigns as prime minister, and is replaced by John Turner.

1974 Bill 22 passes Québec Parliament, making French the official language in the province.

April 17, 1982 Queen Elizabeth II signs the Canada Act.

September 2000 Pierre Trudeau dies of prostate cancer.

81

FURTHER READING

Archbold, Rick. *I Stand for Canada: The Story of the Maple Leaf Flag*. Toronto, Ont.: Macfarlane, Walter & Ross, 2002.

Heathcote, Blake. *Testaments of Honour: Personal Histories from Canada's War Veterans*. Toronto, Ont.: Doubleday Canada Limited, 2002.

Hughes, Susan. *Lester B. Pearson*. Markham, Ont.: Fitzhenry & Whiteside, Limited, 2004.

Kizilos, Peter. *Quebec: Province Divided*. Minneapolis, Minn.: Lerner Publishing Group, 1999.

Sauerwein, Stan. *Pierre Elliott Trudeau: The Fascinating Life of Canada's Most Flamboyant Prime Minister*. Canmore, Alb.: Altitude Publishing, 2004.

Sheehan, Sean. *Greenpeace*. Chicago, Ill.: Raintree Library, 2004.

FOR MORE INFORMATION

Canada's Flag
www.pch.gc.ca/progs/cpsc-ccsp/
sc-cs/df1_e.cfm

CANDU Reactors
www.candu.org/

Controversy surrounding
Canada's Constitution
archives.cbc.ca/300c.asp?id=1-73-1092

Environment Canada
www.ec.gc.ca/envhome.html

Expo 67
www.collectionscanada.ca/expo/
053301_e.html

Front de Libération du Québec
www.marxists.org/history/canada/
quebec/flq/index.htm

Greenpeace Canada
www.greenpeace.ca/e/

Lester Pearson
www.collectionscanada.ca/
primeministers/h4-3350-e.html

Trudeaumania
archives.cbc.ca/IDD-1-74-73/
people/trudeaumania/

White Paper on Indian Affairs
www.ainc-inac.gc.ca/pr/lib/phi/
histlws/cp1969_e.html

Publisher's note:
The Web sites listed on this page were active at the time of publication. The publisher is not responsible for Web sites that have changed their addresses or discontinued operation since the date of publication. The publisher will review and update the Web-site list upon each reprint.

INDEX

PICTURE CREDITS

Centre for Research and Information on Canada: pp. 64–65

Government of Canada: pp. 34–35, 80–81

Liberal Party of Canada: p. 8

National Archives of Canada: pp: 22–23, 24–25, 36, 37, 38, 66, 67, 74–75, 78–79

National Archives of Canada, Myfanwy Pavelic: p. 28

PhotoDisc: pp. 50–51, 54–55, 56–57, 59, 60, 61, 62

PhotoDisc/U.S. Air Force: pp. 52–53

Photos.com: pp. 1, 19, 32, 41 (right), 44–43, 47, 48–49, 69, 76–77

Smithsonian National Air and Space Museum: pp. 14–15

University of Sherbrooke: pp. 42–43

To the best knowledge of the publisher, all other images are in the public domain. If any image has been inadvertently uncredited, please notify Harding House Publishing Service, Vestal, New York 13850, so that rectification can be made for future printings.

BIOGRAPHIES

Sheila Nelson was born in Newfoundland and grew up in both Newfoundland and Ontario. She has written a number of history books for kids and always enjoys the chance to keep learning. She recently earned a master's degree and now lives in Rochester, New York, with her husband and daughter.

SERIES CONSULTANT

Dr. David Bercuson is the Director of the Centre for Military and Strategic Studies at the University of Calgary. His writings on modern Canadian politics, Canadian defense and foreign policy, and Canadian military, among other topics, have appeared in academic and popular publications. Dr. Bercuson is the author, coauthor, or editor of more than thirty books, including *Confrontation at Winnipeg: Labour, Industrial Relations, and the General Strike* (1990), *Colonies: Canada to 1867* (1992), *Maple Leaf Against the Axis, Canada's Second World War* (1995), and *Christmas in Washington: Roosevelt and Churchill Forge the Alliance* (2005). He has also served as historical consultant for several film and television projects, and provided political commentary for CBC radio and television and CTV television. In 1989, Dr. Bercuson was elected a fellow of the Royal Society of Canada. In 2004, Dr. Bercuson received the Vimy Award, sponsored by the Conference of Defence Association Institute, in recognition of his significant contributions to Canada's defense and the preservation of the Canadian democratic principles.